The Giraffe
WHO FOUND
Its Spots

Never change who you are to fit in.
Wear your spots with pride and you
will find your way in life.

It's hard being a giraffe...

I stick out everywhere I go.

I tried to fit in with the other animals to make friends...

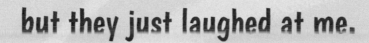

but they just laughed at me.

I tried to show the monkeys that I have
a tail like them....

but they just swung away from me.

I tried to show the cheetahs that
I had spots like them

and could run really fast like them...

but they just ran away from me.

I tried to show the ostriches that I could stick my head in the sand like them ...

but they just flapped away from me.

I tried to show the elephants that I could curl like them...

but they wanted nothing to do with me.

I tried to show the rhinos that I had a horn like them...

but they just charged into me.

I tried to show the flamingos that I could stand like them...

but they just flew away from me.

It's hopeless... no one wants to be my friend.

The animals continue to sing
and dance late into the night.

Wow! The party is incredible now with the moonlight shining down!

This has been the best party ever thanks to you!

Check out our other great books!

Available on Amazon

Made in the USA
Middletown, DE
24 September 2022